DRAGON MASTERS

SONG OF THE POISON DRAGON

BY

TRACEY WEST

ILLUSTRATED BY

DAMIEN JONES

SCHOLASTIC INC.

DRAGON MASTERS

Read All the Adventures

More books coming soon!

TABLE OF CONTENTS

A TALE OF TWO KATIES:

This book is for my sister, Katie Noll,
for all the stories we wove together growing up.
And many thanks to Katie Carella,
who is a genuine wizard of editing. -TW

Library of Congress Cataloging-in-Publication Data
West, Tracey, 1965- author.
Song of the poison dragon / by Tracey West ; illustrated by Damien Jones. — First edition.
pages cm. — (Dragon masters ; 5)
Summary: Petra, the newest dragon master, is scared to death of the Hydra dragon she is supposed to bond with—but when the Hydra accidentally poisons the King, and then her fellow dragon master, Drake, she must find a way to connect with her dragon, because only the Hydra's song can cure them.
ISBN 0-545-91387-X (pbk. : alk. paper) — ISBN 0-545-91388-8 (hardcover : alk. paper) 1. Dragons—Juvenile fiction. 2. Magic—Juvenile fiction. 3. Fear—Juvenile fiction. 4. Poisons—Juvenile fiction. 5. Singing—Juvenile fiction. [1. Dragons—Fiction. 2. Magic—Fiction. 3. Fear—Fiction. 4. Poisons—Fiction. 5. Singing—Fiction.] I. Jones, Damien, illustrator. II. Title. III. Series: West, Tracey, 1965- Dragon Masters ; 5.
PZ7.W51937So 2016
813.54—dc23
[Fic] 2015027415

ISBN 978-0-545-91388-1 (hardcover) / ISBN 978-0-545-91387-4 (paperback)

10 9 8 7 6 5 4 3 2 1 16 17 18 19 20

Printed in China 38
First edition, May 2016
Illustrated by Damien Jones
Edited by Katie Carella
Book design by Jessica Meltzer

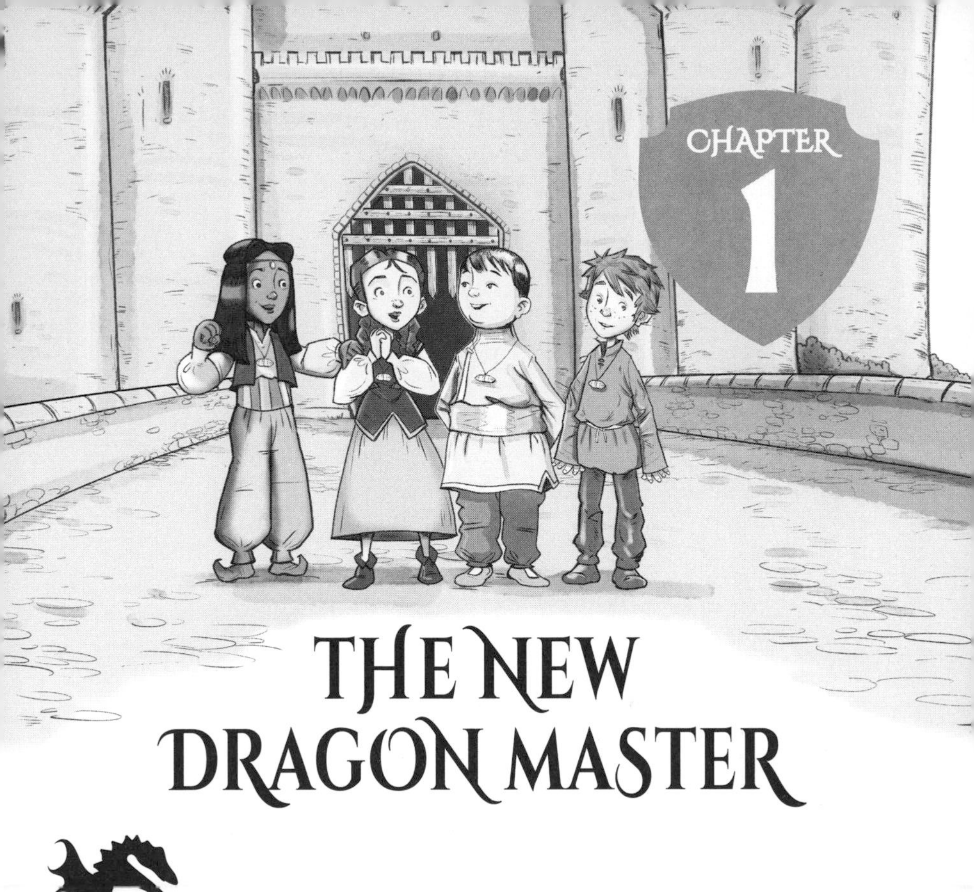

THE NEW DRAGON MASTER

Drake looked out at the crowd of people waiting by the castle gates. It seemed like everyone in the Kingdom of Bracken was there! It was a special day. The new Dragon Master was coming!

Drake stood with the other Dragon Masters—Ana, Rori, and Bo—in front of the castle.

Drake turned to the wizard standing near them. “Griffith, did the Dragon Stone tell you what the new Dragon Master will be like?” he asked.

Griffith shook his head. “All I know is that her name is Petra. She comes from the southern lands. And she is eight years old, like all of you.”

Each of the Dragon Masters had been chosen by the magical Dragon Stone. The stone chose children who could connect with dragons. So far, it had chosen four children from all over the world to live in King Roland’s castle. There, Griffith taught them how to work with their dragons.

Now there was a new dragon at the castle. She was a hydra, a dragon with four heads. An evil wizard named Maldred had attacked the kingdom, riding the hydra. Maldred was sent to the Wizard's Council prison. And the Dragon Stone had chosen a Dragon Master for the hydra.

"Petra will be here any minute!" said red-haired Rori. "I wonder what she will be like! What if she's mean?"

"Why would she be mean?" asked Bo.

"Well, the hydra shoots poison," said Rori. "And poison isn't nice."

In the battle with Maldred, the hydra had shot poison from her four mouths. Her liquid poison could melt rocks! And her poison mist had stung the wing of Rori's dragon, Vulcan.

"Just because the hydra shoots poison doesn't make her a mean dragon," Drake said. "That's her power, like how each of our dragons has a different power."

"Right," agreed Ana. "The hydra's heart is good, and I think Petra will be good, too."

"Look!" Bo cried.

Drake saw horses coming down the road. The crowd started to get excited. Some people waved flags with dragons painted on them. Little kids played with wooden dragon toys along the side of the road.

Drake remembered the first day he had come to the castle. One of the king's soldiers had scooped him up on a horse. That had been scary!

I wonder if the new Dragon Master feels scared? Drake thought.

The crowd cheered as the horses stopped at the gates. A soldier helped a young girl down from one of them.

"That must be Petra," Bo whispered to Drake.

Petra wore a long blue dress with brown leather shoes. She had blond curly hair. Her bright-green eyes stared out at the crowd and up at the castle.

The crowd got quiet. Everyone was waiting to hear what the new Dragon Master would say . . .

Petra shivered.

"Is it always this cold here?" she asked.

PETRA KNOWS IT ALL

Drake, Rori, Bo, and Ana walked up to Petra.

"It's fall here," Drake explained. "That's when it starts getting colder."

"We don't have *fall* where I'm from," Petra said, like there was something bad about fall.

"Just wait! It gets even colder in the winter," Rori snapped.

Ana took Petra's hand. "I am from the Land of Pyramids. It's warm there all the time, too. You will get used to the cold like I did."

Griffith clapped. "Come! Let's bring Petra inside."

One of the soldiers turned to the crowd. "Back to the fields!" he yelled.

The Dragon Masters and Griffith walked into the castle. Petra talked the whole way.

"This is the castle? It's so gray and gloomy. Where are the white columns? Where is the gold?" she asked. Petra didn't wait for anyone to answer her questions. She just kept asking them. "That's a tall tower. How tall is it? Can you see the whole kingdom from up there?"

They walked down a hall to a wood door. A guard named Simon opened it for them.

"Petra, we will answer your questions soon," Griffith said. "First, though, we will show you the Training Room and the Dragon Caves. Then we'll take you to your room."

Griffith led them down the long staircase into the Training Room. Torches flickered on the walls.

"It's dark down here," Petra said.

"This is the Training Room, where we work with our dragons," Drake explained.

Bo pointed to a locked room. "That's Griffith's workshop."

"And that's our classroom," said Ana, pointing to the room next to it. "It's filled with books about dragons."

"We can read boring *books* anytime," said Rori. "You must be dying to meet your dragon. Let's go!"

"The books sound interesting," said Petra. But Rori pulled her toward the Dragon Caves.

Rori stopped in front of Vulcan's cave.

"This is Vulcan," Rori said, smiling. The red dragon showed off by spreading his wings.

"A Fire Dragon," said Petra. "He can shoot a flame as tall as a tree."

"How do you know that?" Rori asked.

"*Everybody* knows that," Petra replied.

Then Ana led her to another Dragon Cave.

"This is my Sun Dragon, Kepri," said Ana, pointing to the white dragon inside.

"Does Kepri's Moon Dragon twin live here, too?" Petra asked.

"You know about Moon Dragons?" Ana asked, her dark eyes wide.

"Doesn't everyone?" Petra said.

Bo waved to Petra. "Come meet Shu, my Water Dragon," he said, leading her to a blue dragon with shimmering scales. "She can—"

"She can cure dark-magic spells," said Petra, before Bo could finish.

Drake and Bo looked at each other, frowning. *What a know-it-all!* Drake thought.

Drake walked over to Worm's cave. His brown, legless dragon looked up when Drake got near.

"This is Worm," said Drake. "He's an Earth Dragon. But you probably already know his power."

"He can move things with his mind," said Petra.

Rori put her hands on her hips. "How do you know all this?" she asked.

"A long time ago, a member of my family was a dragon expert," answered Petra. "His name was Cosmo. I have heard many stories about Cosmo and dragons. Cosmo even tamed a four-headed dragon. He kept it as a pet!"

"And now, Petra, it is time for you to meet *your* dragon," said Griffith.

FOUR HEADS

"Yes, of course. I should meet my dragon," said Petra.

Griffith took something out of his pocket: a chain with a green stone hanging from it.

"First, here is a piece of the Dragon Stone," said Griffith. "Every Dragon Master has one. This will help you connect with your dragon."

Petra slipped the stone around her neck.

"*Ooh*, it matches your eyes," said Ana.

"Don't worry if you don't connect with the hydra at first," said Drake. He remembered that he and Worm did not connect right away. "It may take time, but it will happen."

"Did you say *hydra*? My dragon is a hydra?" Petra asked, and her eyes were wide.

"Yes, a four-headed dragon," said Rori. "But that Cosmo guy tamed one, so it should be no problem for you, right?"

Drake thought he saw a look of worry flash across Petra's face. But then it was gone.

"What are we waiting for? Let's go see my hydra!" she said.

Griffith led the Dragon Masters to a fifth cave covered with wood bars.

"Here she is," Griffith said, opening the gate. The hydra raised all four necks. She had shiny green scales, big wings, and bright-yellow eyes.

Petra took a step back. "Yup, four heads, they're all there," she said. "That's good. Can I see my room now?"

"Don't you want to talk to your dragon?" asked Bo.

"You need to name her," said Rori.

Petra shook her head. "*Everybody* knows you can't name a hydra right away," she said. "You have to wait."

"Wait for what?" Drake asked.

Petra didn't answer. "Can somebody please show me my room?" she asked again.

"We will eat first," Griffith said. "You must be hungry."

"Fine," Petra said, and then she marched off without another look at the hydra.

The other Dragon Masters looked at Griffith.

"We must give her time," said Griffith. "Now, let's go eat!"

A MESSAGE FROM THE KING

Drake caught up to Petra.

"You'll like dinner," he said as they walked. "The food is really good."

"I *am* hungry," Petra said, entering the dining room.

The table was full of plates piled high with roast beef, chicken, potatoes, carrots, and bread. Petra stood still while the others quickly took their seats. She stared at the table.

"Where are the chickpeas? And the olives? And the figs?" she asked.

"I don't know what a fig is. But we have roast beef," Drake said.

Petra sighed. "My family doesn't eat meat," she said.

Griffith waved to her. "Come and sit with us, please."

Just as Petra sat down, Griffith got a twinkle in his eye. He pointed a finger at the potatoes. One of them floated up and landed on Petra's plate! Petra's eyes widened at the sight of the magic.

"The potatoes are delicious," Griffith said.

Drake watched Petra poke at her potato with her fork.

"Petra, I was thinking," Bo said. "Maybe the Dragon Stone chose you for the hydra because of Cosmo."

"Maybe taming hydras is a talent that runs in your family," Ana added.

"Maybe," Petra said, not looking up.

Then they heard a sound on the stairs. Simon the guard marched in.

"I have a message for you, wizard," he said. "King Roland wants to see all of the Dragon Masters and their beasts tomorrow. In the courtyard."

"Why not in the Training Room?" Griffith asked.

"Queen Rose is coming to visit. The king wants to show off his new dragon outside," the guard replied, and then he left.

"Tomorrow?" Petra asked with a squeak in her voice. "But I have not even worked with the hydra yet. Everyone knows it takes time to get to know a dragon."

"I agree it is too soon. But we must obey the king, " Griffith said. "And his friend Queen Rose is very nice. You will like meeting her."

Petra frowned. She ate a few bites of her potato and then pushed her plate away.

"I'm done," she said. "May I please go to my room now?"

Griffith nodded. "Of course. We will see you at breakfast."

"I'll show you to your room," Ana offered.

The two girls left, and the other Dragon Masters looked at one another.

"I don't think Petra is fitting in very well," Rori blurted out.

"Nonsense," said Griffith. "She fits in fine. Give her time."

Bo leaned over to Drake. "What do you think?" he whispered.

Drake hated to say it. It hadn't been easy for him when he first came to the castle. But he had been excited to be there and to meet the dragons. Petra didn't seem excited at all.

"I'm not sure she belongs," Drake whispered.

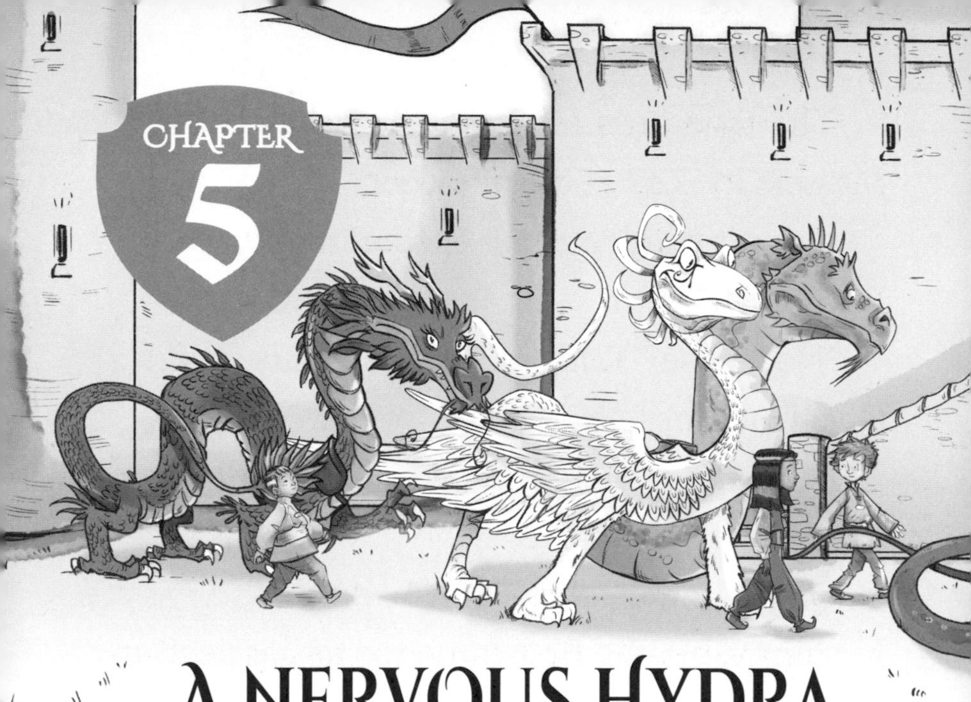

A NERVOUS HYDRA

The next day, the Dragon Masters brought their dragons to the courtyard as the king had asked.

"Are you sure we have to do this?" Petra asked, walking with the hydra behind her.

"This won't take long," Griffith promised her. "The king just wants to show off your dragon to Queen Rose."

Drake was happy to be outside with Worm. His Earth Dragon slid across the grass beside him. Shu was next to Bo. Kepri walked with Ana, and Vulcan stomped along behind Rori.

"Did you name your hydra yet?" Rori asked Petra.

"Not yet," Petra replied. "You can't rush these things."

King Roland stood in the courtyard, waiting for them. He was tall, with a bushy red beard. Queen Rose, from the Kingdom of Arkwood, stood next to him. She had a kind face and she wore her hair in two long braids.

Behind them, the king's guards were trying to hold back a crowd of villagers.

"I thought we were just going to meet the king and Queen Rose," said Petra. "Why are so many people here?"

“Word must have got out that the dragons would be outside,” Drake guessed. “The villagers have been excited about the dragons ever since they found out about them.”

King Roland came toward them. “Good morning, Griffith!” he said in his booming voice. “Thank you for bringing the dragons.”

The king walked up to the hydra and then turned to Queen Rose. “See? This new dragon has four heads!” he said. “Just like I told you!”

“This is an amazing dragon,” the queen said. “What can she do?”

Griffith started to talk about the hydra. Two little kids ran past the guards. They each had a dragon toy—a dragon head with a long ribbon tail, attached to a stick. They chased each other around the courtyard, waving the sticks.

The hydra’s four mouths frowned as the kids got closer. Her two front feet started to paw the ground. Drake noticed it. But Petra had her back to the hydra.

Then Drake's Dragon Stone started to glow. That sometimes meant Worm was trying to tell him something. Now he could hear Worm inside his head.

Petra must calm the hydra. She must pat her heads right away.

Drake nodded at Worm.

Drake ran up to Petra. "Petra, your dragon is nervous," he whispered to her. "You must pat her heads."

"Pat her heads?" Petra asked. She looked pale.

The hydra started to snort and pant.

"Is something wrong with this dragon?" King Roland asked.

"Petra, do it now," Drake urged.

"You don't pat a hydra's heads," she said. "You're supposed to—um—pat their tails. *Everyone* knows that."

She moved to the back of the hydra, reached out, and patted her tail.

"*Aaaiieeee!*" the hydra cried out.

One of the heads reared back—the head closest to King Roland. A light mist sprayed from the head's mouth.

King Roland fell to the ground!

CHAPTER 6

POISON!

Everything happened at once.

Queen Rose ran to King Roland's side. His skin was starting to turn green. "Somebody help him!" she cried.

Petra's eyes were wide with shock.

The villagers started to yell.

"That beast hurt the king!"

"Stop that dragon!"

The villagers tried to push past the guards.

Drake looked at Worm. "Get the hydra inside, quick!" he said.

Worm nodded. He touched the hydra with the end of his tail. Worm's body glowed green.

Then Worm and the hydra disappeared.

"Back to the Training Room! Hurry!" Griffith told the Dragon Masters. "I will see to the king."

The Dragon Masters raced back to the caves with their dragons.

When the Dragon Masters reached the classroom, Rori marched up to Petra. "What did you do?"

"I don't know!" Petra shouted.

"We know that the hydra's poison is strong," said Bo. "The king must have breathed in the mist and it made him sick."

"Is there a cure?" Rori asked Petra.

"I . . . I don't know," Petra admitted.

"But I thought you knew *everything*," Rori said, and Petra's face turned red.

"Can't Shu cure him—like she cured Emperor Song?" Ana asked.

Bo shook his head. "Shu can only undo dark-magic spells. Not poison."

"Maybe the answer is in a book," Drake guessed.

Drake, Rori, Bo, and Ana ran to the bookshelf.

"Look for books about hydras," Bo said, scanning the titles. "And Poison Dragons."

Drake glanced behind him and saw Petra standing by the doorway.

"Come help us," he said. "There are lots of books."

Petra joined them. The Dragon Masters each took a book. They were all reading when Griffith returned.

"How is the king?" Bo asked.

Griffith frowned. "Very ill, I'm afraid. He has a fever and has not woken up. We must find a cure for the hydra's poison."

"I found something," Ana said, pointing to a page in her book. "It says here that the hydra can cure someone hurt by its own poison. *Hmmm* . . . But it does not say how."

"Interesting," said Griffith. "Perhaps Petra can connect with the hydra to find the answer."

"But the hydra doesn't *want* to connect with me," Petra said. "Look what happened when I touched her!"

"Petra, you must still try," said Griffith. "You are a Dragon Master now. The king needs you."

Everyone looked at Petra.

"I'll do it," she said quietly. Then her voice got louder, like she was trying hard to be brave. "I am a Dragon Master, just like all of you!"

CHAPTER 7

NEWS FROM THE VILLAGE

Petra marched off toward the Dragon Caves. Everyone hurried behind her. They were all sharing ideas about how she could befriend the hydra.

"You might want to polish her scales," said Bo. "Shu likes that very much."

"Vulcan likes it when I rub under his chin," said Rori. "You should try that."

Ana chimed in. "You could give her a name."

"Worm loves apples," said Drake. "Maybe give the hydra a snack."

Petra opened the gate to her dragon's cave. She took one step inside. Then she looked back at the others.

"I don't need to do any of those things," Petra said. "All I have to do is close my eyes and think hard about my dragon. Everyone knows that's how you form a connection."

"But—" Rori started to say.

Griffith held up a hand to silence her. "Every dragon is different," he said. "So is every Dragon Master. Let Petra try it her way."

Petra closed her eyes. Her Dragon Stone started to glow pale green.

"Can you hear the hydra in your head?" Rori asked, tapping her foot.

"I'm trying!" snapped Petra.

Then Simon the guard ran in, out of breath.

"I have news from the village," he said. "People have turned against the dragons now that King Roland is sick. They are saying that the dragons should be locked up somewhere far away from the kingdom!"

The Dragon Masters gasped.

"Oh dear," said Griffith. "Thank you for warning us."

Simon nodded and ran off.

Rori balled her hands into fists. "*Nobody* is taking Vulcan away from me!" she cried.

"This is awful," said Bo.

"It is terrible that King Roland got sick," added Ana. "But it wasn't the hydra's fault!"

"I can't think in here," Petra blurted out. She pushed past the Dragon Masters.

"Are you just going to let her leave?" Rori asked Griffith.

"I cannot force Petra to connect with her dragon," he replied. "I hope she will come back soon. But until then, we must keep looking for a cure. Back to the books, Dragon Masters! I will go see if the Dragon Stone can help us."

He turned to Drake. "Can you go check on Petra?"

Drake nodded and ran out of the Dragon Caves. Part of him was angry with Petra. But he was also worried about her. *She is far from home. I'm sure she thinks this is all her fault,* he thought. *She must feel terrible—especially now that all of our dragons are in danger!*

CHAPTER 8

THE TRUTH COMES OUT

Drake walked up the twisty staircase to the tower where the Dragon Masters slept. Petra's door was open. He poked his head inside.

"Petra?" he asked.

Petra sat on the edge of her bed, looking down at her lap.

"What happened to King Roland isn't your fault," Drake said.

"But it is!" she cried. "I should have patted the hydra's heads—like you said—to calm her down. But I lied and said I should pat her tails instead. I-I-I was afraid."

Drake sat down next to her. "Afraid of what?"

"I'm terrified of my dragon," Petra admitted. "She's got four heads and shoots poison!"

"But you're a Dragon Master," Drake said. "You can connect with her."

Petra shook her head.

"How can I connect with her when I can't even touch her?" Petra asked. "Everybody in my family expects me to be good with dragons, like Cosmo was. But I'm not!"

"When I first came here, I was afraid, too. Vulcan shot fire at me!" Drake said. "The dragons were all so big and scary-looking. But they're really friendly. I'll show you. Let's go back to the hydra."

"Are you sure I won't get hurt?" Petra asked.

"The hydra only shot poison at the king because she got scared," said Drake. "We'll take it nice and slow. And don't forget about your Dragon Stone. It will help you connect with your dragon."

Petra took a deep breath. "Okay. I'll try."

They went back down to the hydra's cave.

Drake opened the gate. "Ask her to come out," he said.

Petra faced her dragon. "Can you please come out?"

The hydra slowly stepped out of her cave.

"Now ask her to follow us," said Drake.

"Please follow us, hydra," Petra said.

The big green dragon followed Drake and Petra to the Training Room. The other Dragon Masters looked up from their books.

Drake reached out and gently stroked one of the hydra's heads.

"See? She won't hurt you," he said. He reached out a hand to Petra. "Come on, we can do it together."

Petra placed her hand in Drake's. Drake could feel that it was shaking. Together, they pet the hydra.

The hydra began to make a strange sound.

Purrrrrrrrrr. . .

"Is my dragon purring?" asked Petra. "She sounds like my kitten back home!"

"She sounds happy," said Drake, smiling.

Petra looked up at the hydra. "Can you help King Roland?" she asked.

The Dragon Stone around her neck started to glow—but only for a second. Then it went dark.

"It's not working!" Petra cried.

The others came out of the classroom.

"Connecting takes time," said Bo.

"That's a good start," added Ana.

Even Rori chimed in. "Don't give up now."

Petra nodded. "You're right. And thank you, Drake, for helping me to not be so afraid." She stroked the hydra's neck.

Purrrrrrrrrrr . . .

Petra tried to connect with the hydra all afternoon. But she didn't have any luck. Drake, Rori, Bo, and Ana didn't find any clues in their books, either.

At the end of the day, Griffith came out of his workshop.

"It's late, everyone," Griffith said. "Time to get some sleep."

"But what about the king?" Ana asked.

"He is still sick with a fever," Griffith replied. "I will keep trying to find an answer."

Petra looked at Drake. "You said it would take time," she said. "I just hope I can connect with the hydra in time to save the king!"

CHAPTER 9

THE WRONG DRAGON MASTER

The next morning, Petra knocked on Drake and Bo's door before breakfast.

"Come in," said Drake with a yawn.

"Could you take me to see the hydra?" Petra asked. Her green eyes shone eagerly. "I want to start connecting with my dragon right away!"

Drake's stomach grumbled. "Before we eat breakfast?"

"I grabbed these from the kitchen." Petra held up some bread and cheese. "Let's go!"

Bo opened his eyes long enough to see Drake go off with Petra. The two hurried down the stairs to the Training Room. As they got near Griffith's Workshop, they heard voices. Drake and Petra stopped to listen.

"Please, Griffith, there must be some way to help him," a woman's voice said.

"That sounds like Queen Rose," Drake whispered to Petra.

"The hydra is the key to healing the king," said Griffith. "But we won't know *how* until her Dragon Master connects with her. Petra simply is not ready."

"But she *must* be ready!" said Queen Rose. "Can't another Dragon Master make the connection?"

"It doesn't work that way," Griffith explained. "The Dragon Stone has chosen Petra."

"Then the Dragon Stone should choose someone else!" the queen said. "The king's life is at stake."

They heard Griffith sigh. "Let me check the Dragon Stone again," he said.

Drake peeked into the workshop. Griffith was leaning over the Dragon Stone. The stone sat in a wooden box carved with pictures of dragons. The Dragon Masters' stones had come from this Dragon Stone.

Griffith gazed into the shining green gem. He frowned. "I am sorry, Your Majesty," he said. "The Dragon Stone is cloudy. It has been acting strangely lately. Sometimes clouds appear. Other times it glows brightly and fades."

Drake heard a rumbling sound outside the castle.

"This Dragon Stone must not be working as it should," said Queen Rose. "It must have chosen the wrong Dragon Master!"

Drake looked at Petra. She was biting her lower lip.

"Petra, I'm sure that—" Drake began, but he stopped.

The rumbling sound was clearer. It was the villagers, chanting.

"Send the dragons away!" they yelled.

SEND THE DRAGONS AWAY!

Rori, Bo, and Ana came running down the stairs. They almost bumped into Drake and Petra.

"There's an angry crowd outside the castle!" Rori cried.

"A *very* angry crowd," added Bo.

"We can't let them send the dragons away!" said Ana.

Griffith and Queen Rose came out of the workshop. The Dragon Masters bowed to the queen.

"I must return to King Roland's side," Queen Rose said. "Griffith, please think about what I said."

Griffith nodded. "I will do everything I can."

As soon as the queen left, Griffith turned to the Dragon Masters. "Stay calm," he said. "How large is this angry mob?"

“There are more people by the castle gate than I’ve ever seen,” said Rori. “The guards are trying to hold them back.”

“What if they break into the castle?” Ana asked. “What if they take away the dragons?”

“Nobody is taking the dragons anywhere,” Griffith said.

“I’m so sorry!” Petra blurted out. “This is all my fault!”

Then she ran off toward the Dragon Caves.

"Let her go," said Rori. "She's not going to help us anyway."

"That's not true," said Drake. "She's been trying to help. She's close to connecting with the hydra."

"Until that happens, we need to protect our dragons," Rori argued. "Vulcan can shoot fire at the villagers to scare them."

"Rori, you must understand: The villagers are afraid. They are worried about their king," Griffith said. "Scaring them *more* won't help them. We need a peaceful solution to this problem. Let me find out exactly what's going on. You four, get back to the books!"

The Dragon Masters rushed to the classroom. Suddenly, Drake's Dragon Stone glowed. He heard Worm in his head.

Petra has run away with the hydra!

PETRA'S GOOD-BYE

Drake ran to Worm's cave.

"Where's Petra? Where's the hydra?" Drake asked Worm.

Drake waited for Worm to answer. But there was only a fuzzy sound in his mind. Drake looked at his Dragon Stone. The light was flickering on and off.

That's strange, thought Drake. "Worm?" he asked.

Worm's body started to glow, and Drake knew what that meant. He touched Worm's head.

A green light flashed. A second later, they landed in the Valley of Clouds. The valley was hidden behind the castle, tucked between mountains.

Petra was halfway across the valley. She was trying to climb up on the hydra's back. Drake thought the dragon looked worried.

"Petra! What are you doing?" Drake called to her.

"I'm going home," she replied. "The hydra can fly me there. Queen Rose is right. The Dragon Stone chose the wrong master. But maybe someone else in my family can connect with the hydra and help the king."

"But *you're* the hydra's Dragon Master!" Drake said, running over to her.

"Sorry, Drake," Petra said. "I will send the hydra back with her *real* Dragon Master as soon as I can. Good-bye!"

She started to climb up onto the hydra.

Drake ran over and grabbed her arm.

“Petra, no!” Drake cried. “You don’t have a saddle! You don’t even know how to ride a dragon! You could get hurt!”

Griffith and the other Dragon Masters ran into the valley.

"Petra, stop!" Griffith called out.

"Drake! We saw you run out, and we knew something was wrong!" Ana cried.

Drake turned toward the others – and lost his grip on Petra's arm. She slipped off the hydra's back and tried to break her fall by grabbing the hydra's tail.

"*Aaaaaieeeee!*" the hydra cried out.

One of the hydra's heads reared back. A mist of green poison shot from her mouth. Drake saw the shimmering green cloud shooting toward his face!

Then everything went black.

THE HYDRA'S SONG

"Drake, no!" Petra yelled. She ran to Drake and knelt by him.

"He's hurt!" Bo cried.

Worm quickly crawled to Drake's side. Bo, Rori, Ana, and Griffith raced along with him.

Drake was lying in the grass. His skin was a strange green color.

"We must bring him inside," said Griffith.

"We'll help you, Drake," Ana said.

"He's been poisoned! Just like the king!" Rori exclaimed.

Petra started to cry. "I am so sorry," she said. Tears flowed down her cheeks. They dripped onto her Dragon Stone.

Bo pointed to Petra's Dragon Stone. "Look!"

The stone was glowing a bright, deep green. Petra looked down at it. Her eyes got wide. "I hear voices in my head!" she said. "Four voices. The hydra says she can help Drake."

Then a beautiful sound filled the air.

Everyone turned to see the hydra slowly walking toward Drake. All four of her heads were raised. Each head sang a different tone, but they all blended together.

As the hydra got closer, her song became louder.

"It's beautiful," said Griffith.

"It makes me think of water flowing over rocks," added Bo.

The green color slowly left Drake's skin. His eyes fluttered open.

"What happened?" Drake asked.

He sat up.

"The hydra's mist poisoned you," Petra told him. "But then she healed you with her song."

"I feel fine," Drake said. "Wait! That means you connected with her!"

"Yes, but I'm just glad you're all right," Petra said. "I should have listened to you, Drake. I never should have tried to fly off like that. I'm sorry."

Drake smiled at her. "It's okay."

Rori grabbed Petra's arm. "This is all very nice, but you've got to hurry!" she said.

"Petra, you must save the king!" added Griffith.

TOO LATE?

Worm began to glow green. Drake stood up.

"Petra, hold my hand," Drake told her. "Then touch the hydra with your other hand."

Petra nodded. Now Drake, Petra, and the hydra were all linked with Worm.

A green light flashed. Seconds later, they landed inside King Roland's bedroom. Queen Rose was sitting beside King Roland's bed. She jumped up when she saw Drake, Petra, Worm, and the hydra.

"Guards!" she yelled.

Drake stepped forward and bowed. "Please, Your Majesty. We know how to help the king. The hydra can heal him."

"*Hmm*," the queen said. "Griffith did say that the hydra might be the key to healing the king."

Two guards ran in. They pointed spears at the dragons. Queen Rose held up her hand.

"Lower your weapons," the queen said. "But stand your ground. If the dragons try to harm the king, take action."

Petra held the Dragon Stone in her hands.

"You can do it," Drake told her, and she nodded.

Petra closed her eyes tightly. "Please," she said to the hydra. "Please sing your song."

The Dragon Stone began to glow. Then the hydra started to sing. Her beautiful song filled the room. Drake and Petra anxiously watched the king. He didn't look any better.

Griffith rushed into the room just as the song faded.

“It didn’t work,” Petra told Griffith.

Griffith put a hand on her shoulder. “Drake was only sick for a few minutes before the hydra healed him,” he said. “Perhaps the king’s healing will take longer.”

Queen Rose nodded. “His hand already feels cooler to my touch,” she said. “That gives me hope. And before this, I had none at all. So thank you.”

Griffith turned to Drake and Petra.

"The king needs peace and quiet," he said. "Return the dragons to their caves. Then eat dinner and get to bed. I will stay here to watch over the king."

"But what about the angry mob outside?" Drake asked.

"The guards will keep order," Griffith said. "We must not worry."

Drake nodded. He reached for Petra's hand. Drake touched Worm. A green light flashed. Then they landed back at the Dragon Caves.

ZERA

Toot-toot-toot-toooooot!

The sound of trumpets filled the air early the next morning. Drake and the other Dragon Masters rushed outside, along with everyone else in the castle. Villagers filled the courtyard.

Toot-toot-toot-toooooot!

Trumpet players stood on the king's balcony.

"It sounds like they're going to announce something," said Rori.

"It must be about the king," Petra said, her face pale with worry. "I hope he's all right!"

"All hail King Roland!" the guards shouted.

King Roland stepped onto the balcony with Queen Rose. The crowd began to cheer.

"People of Bracken, I am healed!" the king said loudly. "I am healed by the very dragon that harmed me."

Some people in the crowd began to boo.

"Silence!" ordered the king.

"What happened to me was an accident," the king continued. "Yes, dragons can be dangerous. But our Dragon Masters work hard to train them. I searched the globe for my dragons. I am not giving up on them now—and neither should you!"

Drake smiled. He looked at his friends. They were smiling, too.

"So no more talk against the dragons!" the king said. "I shall not hear it. And now, I must get back to running this kingdom. Good day!"

Queen Rose led him back inside.

Petra threw her arms around Drake. "It worked!" she said. "We saved the king!"

"And all of our dragons are safe again!" said Ana.

Griffith smiled at the Dragon Masters. "Well done, all of you. Especially Petra, our newest Dragon Master. Now let's get to the Valley of Clouds for some training."

The Dragon Masters cheered.

Later that day, the Dragon Masters and their dragons went to the valley with Griffith.

Petra gently stroked one of the hydra's necks.

"I finally have a name for my dragon," she announced. "It's Zera."

"Zera?" asked Ana. "That's pretty."

"It's the name of my kitten back home," said Petra. "The hydra reminds me of her since she also purrs when she is happy."

"Vulcan shoots sparks from his nose when *he's* happy," Rori said with a giggle. The two girls smiled at each other.

Suddenly, Drake heard Worm's voice.

Look up!

Drake pointed to the sky.

A large, dark dragon swooped down. As the dragon got closer, Drake could see his shimmering black scales. He could see the dragon's rider, too: a boy with dark, curly hair.

"It's Heru and Wati!" Drake cried.

CHAPTER 15

THE PRIME DRAGON STONE

That black dragon is Kepri's Moon Dragon twin, right?" Petra asked.

"Right," said Rori. "That's Wati."

Drake turned to Petra. "And Heru is our friend from the Land of Pyramids."

"Kepri became sick so we traveled to the Land of Pyramids to find her twin. Wati healed her," explained Ana.

Everyone ran to Heru as Wati landed in the grass. Kepri quickly flew to Wati's side. He flapped his wings, happy to see his sister.

Heru climbed off Wati's back.

"It's so good to see you again!" said Ana.

Heru hugged Ana, but he wasn't smiling. "I have come because I need your help," he said. He turned to Griffith. "There is something wrong with the prime Dragon Stone."

"The prime Dragon Stone?" asked Drake. "What is that?"

"All of the other Dragon Stones come from the prime stone," replied Griffith. "It is very big and very beautiful. And very hidden."

Heru nodded. "And now it is dying," he said.

"I had a feeling something was wrong," said Griffith. "My stone has been acting strangely."

"I have had some trouble communicating with Worm," Drake added.

"That is why you must come with me," said Heru. "Without the prime stone, Dragon Masters will no longer be able to connect with their dragons!"